HEiDi HECKELBECK
and the Christmas Surprise

By Wanda Coven
Illustrated by Priscilla Burris

LITTLE SIMON
New York London Toronto Sydney New Delhi

LITTLE SIMON
An imprint of Simon & Schuster Children's Publishing Division
1230 Avenue of the Americas, New York, New York 10020
Copyright © 2013 by Simon & Schuster, Inc.
All rights reserved, including the right of reproduction in whole or in part in any form.
LITTLE SIMON is a registered trademark of Simon & Schuster, Inc., and associated colophon is a trademark of Simon & Schuster, Inc.
For information about special discounts for bulk purchases, please contact Simon & Schuster Special Sales at 1-866-506-1949 or business@simonandschuster.com.
The Simon & Schuster Speakers Bureau can bring authors to your live event. For more information or to book an event contact the Simon & Schuster Speakers Bureau at 1-866-248-3049 or visit our website at www.simonspeakers.com.
Manufactured in the United States of America 0813 FFG
First Edition 10 9 8 7 6 5 4 3 2 1
Library of Congress Cataloging-in-Publication Data
Coven, Wanda.
Heidi Heckelbeck and the Christmas surprise / by Wanda Coven ; illustrated by Priscilla Burris. — 1st ed.
p. cm.
Summary: After Heidi borrows her mother's charm bracelet without permission, it gets damaged and she uses magic to try to repair it before her mother finds out, and that is a problem that only Aunt Trudy or Santa can fix.
ISBN 978-1-4424-8124-4 (pbk. : alk. paper) — ISBN 978-1-4424-8125-1 (hardcover : alk. paper) — ISBN 978-1-4424-8126-8 (ebook : alk. paper) [1. Charm bracelets—Fiction. 2. Behavior—Fiction. 3. Witches—Fiction. 4. Magic—Fiction. 5. Christmas—Fiction.] I. Burris, Priscilla, ill. II. Title.
PZ7.C83393Ham 2013
[Fic]—dc23
2012030273

CONTENTS

Chapter 1

A LETTER TO SANTA

Hey, Santa,

It's me, Heidi Heckelbeck. How's it going up there at the North Pole? Hope you had a good year. Mine was very good. I hardly got into trouble! But you probably already know that. By the way, do you really see me when I'm sleeping and know when I'm awake? And are you really magical? Hope you don't mind all the questions.

Now I'd like to talk about Christmas. I only want one thing this year. Can you guess what it is? It's PRINCESS CHARMING by Helen Cranston. Princess

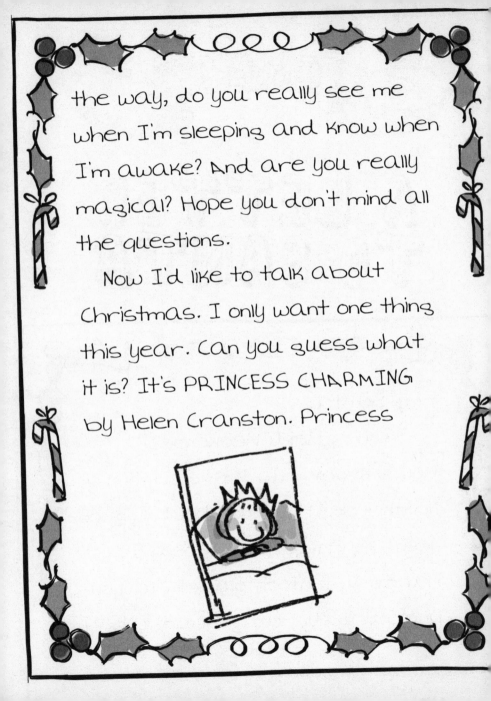

Charming is a witch in disguise. I love that because it reminds me of ME, except for one thing. Princess Charming is a princess and I'm just a regular ol' kid at dumb ol' Brewster Elementary. BOR-ing.

I hope you have good weather for your sleigh ride. Your friend, Heidi

Heidi folded the letter and slipped it into an envelope. Then she addressed it in her neatest handwriting:

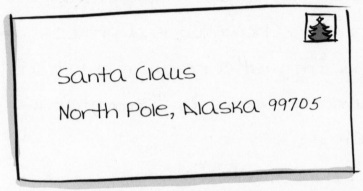

Santa Claus
North Pole, Alaska 99705

Heidi stuck a Christmas tree stamp in the upper right-hand corner. She looked at the envelope. *Hmm . . . it seems boring,* she thought. *I'll have to make it more cheery. I really want Santa to notice my letter.* Heidi opened her desk drawer and took out her

rainbow markers. Then she drew a candy cane, a snowman, and a rein-deer on the envelope.

"Done!" she said triumphantly. "My letter to Santa is ready. Now all I have to do is mail it."

Heidi tingled with excitement. *I hope I get that new book,* she thought. Then she trotted down the hall to find her mom.

TiNY TRiNKETS

Mom stood at her dresser and put on a small hoop earring. Her jewelry box stood open like a treasure chest. Heidi peeked inside. She loved to poke through her mom's jewelry. She waded through the trinkets with one finger and pulled out a silver charm

bracelet. *I've never noticed this before,*
thought Heidi. *It's so beautiful.* Tiny
silver charms hung from a silver link
chain. The bracelet had a pretty silver
toggle clasp.

"Where did you get this?" asked
Heidi, holding the bracelet in her
hand.

Mom looked at the charm bracelet and smiled. "I got that for my tenth birthday," she said. "I collected the charms for years."

Heidi admired each tiny charm.
Some of the charms had movable
parts. Heidi tried each one. She
opened the lid on an itsy-bitsy jack-in-
the-box, and out popped a mini silver
clown. She pushed the clown back
inside. Then she opened a teeny-tiny
sunglasses case and pulled out a wee
pair of sunglasses. She tucked them

back inside. Then she pressed a but-
ton on a mini toaster, and up popped
two slices of toast.

"I LOVE this bracelet," said Heidi.

Mom brushed her hair and looked
at Heidi in the mirror. "It's one of my
favorites," she said. "Someday I'll give
it to you."

"Really?" said Heidi, her eyes

growing wide. "Can I try it on?"

"Sure," Mom said.

Mom wrapped the bracelet around
Heidi's wrist and inserted the toggle
into the loop. Heidi held out her arm
and admired the bracelet.

"I wish I could have it now," Heidi
said.

"How about when you turn ten?"
said Mom. "If I give it to you too soon,
it may slip off your wrist."

Heidi shook the bracelet to see if it
would fall off. It was only a tiny bit
too big. She doubted it would fall off.

"Can't I please have it now?" asked Heidi. "I'll go SO bonkers if I have to wait that long."

"I'll let you try it on once in a while," said Mom. "Then it won't seem like such a long time to wait. But always remember to ask for permission first. Okay?"

Heidi nodded.

Then Henry galloped into the room.

"Yeehaw!" he shouted.

Heidi's younger brother had on a brown leather cowboy hat, a red bandanna, and brown cowboy boots.

Henry tipped his hat. "Howdy, pardners!" he said.

"Howdy!" said Mom.

"Whatever," said Heidi.

Henry noticed the bracelet on Heidi's wrist.

"WHERE did you get that?" asked Henry.

"In Mom's jewelry box," said Heidi.

Henry galloped to Mom's jewelry box and looked inside. He pulled out a long strand of pearls and swung them around on one finger.

"Can I use this as a lasso?" he asked.

Mom caught the twirling pearls in midair.

"Let's find you a piece of rope instead," she said. "Heidi, would you find one for your brother? We have rope in the garage."

"Sure, Mom," said Heidi, taking off the bracelet and placing it carefully into the box. "And then I have to mail my letter to Santa."

"You're only just mailing it NOW?" asked Henry. "I mailed mine in October. I wanted to make sure Santa got mine first."

Heidi rolled her eyes. "Well, la-di-da," she said, pretending not to worry—even though she really did.

Then they raced to the garage.

Chapter 3

FIT FOR A QUEEN

Heidi found a piece of rope on a hook in the garage. She handed it to Henry.

"Don't strangle yourself, pardner," said Heidi.

Henry rolled his eyes.

"Har-dee-har-har," he said.

Henry and Heidi put on their coats

and headed for the mailbox. Heidi popped her letter in and put up the flag. Henry mounted the garden gate as if it were a horse. It was made of logs, so it was easy to straddle. He lifted the metal bar that latched the gate and used it for the reins. Then he bounced up and down and twirled the rope over his head.

"Wahoo!" he shouted.

Heidi folded her arms and watched her brother. She noticed a car com-ing down the street. *Hey, that's the Lancasters' car,* she thought.

"Lucy's here!" she shouted.

Heidi had been expecting Lucy. They had planned a playdate earlier in the week. Heidi ran to greet her friend. Lucy hopped out of the car and waved good-bye to her mother. The girls held hands and jumped up and down. Then they ran into the house.

"Wait for me!" cried Henry as he hopped off the gate and hurried after the girls.

"Let's play dress-up," suggested
Heidi as soon as they got inside.

"Okay," said Lucy.

"No, thanks," said Henry. "I need to
get back to the corral."

Henry galloped to his room, and
the girls headed for the playroom.

Heidi opened the costume trunk and pulled out a red velvet dress with white fur trim.

"I'm going to be the Christmas Queen," she said.

Lucy rummaged around in the trunk and pulled out a white satin dress. It had ruffles around the skirt and sleeves, and sparkly sequins all over.

"And I'll be Princess Snowflake," she said. "She's a winter fairy."

The girls changed
into their dresses.

Heidi put on a bejeweled
tiara. Lucy wrapped a feathery white
boa around her neck and shoulders.

"Here, use this," said Heidi. She
handed Lucy a silver wand.

Then the girls each
slipped on a pair of
glittery high-heeled
shoes.

"You look fabulous, darling," said
Heidi.

"So do you," said Lucy. "Except a
Christmas Queen needs more jewels."

Heidi looked in the trunk. She found some gold bead necklaces and put several strands around her neck. Then she remembered her mother's charm bracelet.

"I'll be right back," said Heidi.

She ran to her parents' room. She popped open Mom's jewelry box and helped herself to the charm bracelet. *I'll just borrow it for a little while,* she thought. *I'll put it right back when I'm done.*

Heidi zipped back to the playroom.

"Look at this!" she said as she held up the bracelet for Lucy to see.

Lucy's eyes lit up. "Wow, that's SO beautiful," she said.

Heidi showed Lucy all the movable charms. Lucy worked each one.

"Can you help me with the toggle?" asked Heidi.

"Sure," Lucy said.

Lucy stuck the silver *T* into the loop. Then Heidi shook her wrist. The charms tinkled.

"And now it's time for the royal Christmas tea," said Heidi in a proper English accent.

"Oh yes," said

Lucy in the same accent. "Let's pre-
pare to have tea."

Lucy and Heidi set out play teacups
and saucers. They filled the little tea-
pot with water. Then they arranged
plastic pastries on a three-tiered
serving tray. They had miniature cup-
cakes, doughnuts, pretzels, pies, and

cookies. Then the Christmas Queen and Princess Snowflake sat at the table and sipped their tea and nibbled the pastries.

"You have a superb pastry chef, Your Royal Highness," said Princess Snowflake.

"Why, thank you, Princess," said the queen.

Then she shook a silver bell with a wooden handle.

"And now it's time to light the royal Christmas tree," said the queen. "Will you do me the honor, Princess?"

"I shall be delighted," said Princess Snowflake.

Lucy waved her sparkly wand. Then Heidi quickly switched on a tabletop Christmas tree. The colored lights

glowed in the evergreen branches.

"Simply magical," said the queen.

Princess Snowflake curtsied.

"Perhaps you could provide us with some royal Christmas snow," said the queen.

"As you wish, Your Highness," said the princess.

Lucy waved her wand again. Then the girls looked out the window. They both squealed with delight.

"Oh my gosh!" cried Heidi. "It worked. It's really snowing!"

Lucy looked at her wand in disbelief. "Wow! How did I do that?"

"You must have a magic wand," said Heidi.

Lucy giggled. "Let's go out and play in the snow."

"Yeah," said Heidi.

The girls wriggled out of their dresses, put on their play clothes, and ran downstairs.

"Henry, it's snowing!" Heidi called on the way down.

Henry darted out of his room and followed the girls.

They bundled up in hats, mittens, and scarves. Then they ran outside into the swirling snow.

Chapter 4

SNOW DAY!

Heidi and Lucy caught snowflakes on the tips of their tongues. Henry scooped a handful of snow and packed a snowball. Then he threw it smack into Heidi's back.

Heidi whirled around and glared at Henry. "Uh, you know what this means," said Heidi.

Henry shook his head.

"This means WAR!"

Henry squealed and ran from Heidi.

Heidi mounded a ball of snow in her mittens and threw it at her brother. It whizzed past his ear. Henry knelt down and made another snowball. This time he threw

it at Lucy. It hit Lucy in the back of the head. She cringed as the slush slid down her neck.

"Get him!" Lucy shouted.

Heidi and Lucy bombarded Henry with snowballs. Henry ducked and ran away. Then he stumbled into the snow. The girls continued to pelt him with snowballs.

"Stop!" begged Henry. "Stop! I surrender!"

Heidi threw one more snowball. It hit Henry right on the bottom. Heidi and Lucy laughed.

"Okay, the war's over," said Heidi.

"Let's make a snowman," suggested Lucy.

"Great idea," Heidi said.

They each began to roll a ball of snow across the yard. The more they

rolled, the bigger the snowballs got.
Heidi's snowball got so big, it wouldn't
budge. "This one will be the base,"
she said.

They used Lucy's ball of snow for
the middle. Henry's snowball became
the head. Heidi found two pieces of
charcoal in the garage for the eyes.
Lucy added twigs for arms. Henry

put his hat and scarf on the snowman. Then they stood and admired their creation. They named him Cool Dude.

"My hands are freezing," said Lucy.

"Same here," Heidi said.

"I'M turning into an icicle," said Henry. "Let's go inside."

Everyone piled into the mudroom

and hung up their wet clothes. Mom made hot chocolate with mini marshmallows and candy cane stirring sticks. She set a bowl of popcorn on the table. Heidi and Lucy stirred their hot chocolate and licked the candy canes. Henry dropped popcorn into his hot chocolate and scooped it out with a spoon.

Heidi and Lucy stared at Henry.

"What?" he said.

"That's so disgusting," Heidi said.

"It's good," said Henry, slurping a piece of soggy popcorn. "You should try it."

Heidi rolled her eyes.

Then the doorbell rang. Mom went to the front door and brought Lucy's mother into the kitchen.

Mrs. Lancaster smiled. "Did you have a fun afternoon?" she asked.

"Did we EVER!" said Lucy.

Lucy told her mother all about the

royal Christmas tea and playing in the snow. Listening to Lucy reminded Heidi of the charm bracelet. She had forgotten all about it when they went out to play in the snow. She looked at her wrist. The bracelet wasn't there! She pushed up her sleeve. No bracelet!

Oh no, Heidi thought. *I lost Mom's charm bracelet!* She didn't say a word. She knew Mom would be very upset with her for taking the bracelet without asking. *I'll have to look for the bracelet after Lucy goes home,* she thought.

Heidi waited for Lucy to finish her hot chocolate. It seemed like Lucy and her mom would never go home. As soon as they were out the door, Heidi ran straight to the playroom.

Chapter 5

SNOWED UNDER

Heidi pulled everything out of the costume trunk. No bracelet. She crawled around on the floor and looked under the table and chairs. No bracelet. She shook the red velvet dress and looked in its sleeves. Still no bracelet. *It must've fallen off outside.*

Heidi slid back into her soggy boots and coat and ran outside. The snowstorm had turned into a blizzard. She sifted back and forth through the snow with her boots. She walked around the snowman. *Maybe it's in the snowman,* Heidi thought. She brushed patches of snow off the snowman. No bracelet. She wandered

around the yard and looked in the driveway.

It's no use, Heidi thought. *I'll never find it beneath all this snow. I'll have to wait until it melts.* Heidi trudged toward the door. She didn't even notice when Dad pulled into the driveway.

He tooted the horn, and Heidi turned around. There was a Christmas tree on top of the car. Heidi ran toward it. At the same time, Henry ran out the front door as he tried to zip his coat.

"The tree!" exclaimed Henry.

"Hey, guys," said Dad as he got

out of the car. "I almost didn't make it home from Andy's Tree Farm in all this snow. Would you give me a hand?"

"Sure," Heidi said.

Heidi and Henry helped Dad untie the tree and shake off the snow. Then they carried it into the house and set

it up in the family room. Mom turned on some Christmas music. Then Dad swirled strings of lights around and around the tree. Heidi opened the boxes of ornaments. Mom had wrapped each ornament in tissue paper for safekeeping. Heidi and Henry never knew which one they

were going to unwrap. They loved
to announce each ornament as they
unwrapped it.

"I got the gingerbread house!" said
Heidi.

"I got the Frog Prince!" Henry said.

"I got the skier!" Mom said.

"Now I got the pickle!" said Heidi.

They unwrapped nutcrackers, sleds, crystal snowflakes, glittery stars, skates, and dancing Santas.

"We sure have collected a lot of orna-ments over the years," said Dad.

"It reminds me of all the charms I collected for my charm bracelet," said Mom.

She looked at Heidi.

Heidi gulped. *Why did Mom have to mention the charm bracelet?* she

wondered. It made her feel terrible.
Mom will be so unhappy if she finds
out it's missing. Heidi looked out the
window. The snow had gotten even
deeper. *I am SO doomed,* she thought.

Chapter 6

SQUiSH!
SQUASH!

Heidi woke up the next morning and opened the blinds. The sun sparkled on the fresh snow. It was well over a foot deep. *There's no way I'll find the charm bracelet today,* she thought.

Heidi and Henry got ready for school and headed for the bus stop.

The snowplow had left steep snow-
banks on either side of the driveway.
Heidi spotted something in the tire
tracks. She stooped down and lifted
something from the snow. Heidi

gasped. *The charm bracelet!* Then she took a closer look. Most of the charms

had been crushed by the snowplow. *Oh no! NOW what am I going to do?* she wondered. Heidi quickly slipped the bracelet into her backpack. Then she

looked around for Henry. He was on top of a snowbank.

"Come on!" Heidi shouted to him. "We'll be late for the bus!"

Henry slid down the snowbank. Then they raced to the bus stop.

Heidi found Lucy as soon as she got to her classroom.

"I have AWFUL news," said Heidi.

"What's wrong?" Lucy asked.

"I lost my mom's charm bracelet in the snow yesterday," said Heidi. "It must've slipped off."

"You're kidding!" cried Lucy.

"It gets worse," said Heidi.

Before Heidi could tell Lucy the rest of her story, Melanie Maplethorpe— better known as Smell-a-nie—butted in. She had been listening in as usual.

"What did you lose, weirdo?" Melanie asked. "Your brain?"

Heidi whirled around and looked at Melanie.

Melanie had a hand on her hip and a snicker on her face.

Heidi got tongue-tied. Melanie always made her feel uncomfortable.

"Mind your own business," said Lucy. Then she linked arms with Heidi, and they walked to the reading corner.

"Thanks," said Heidi.

Lucy nodded. "So what happened?" she asked.

"I found the bracelet in our drive-way," said Heidi. "But it had gotten smooshed by the snowplow."

Heidi pulled the bracelet out of her pocket and dangled it in front of Lucy. Lucy clapped her hand over her

mouth. "Oh no!" she cried. "What are you going to do?"

"I'm going to try to fix it after school," said Heidi.

"Not to be mean," said Lucy, "but it would take a magician to fix that bracelet."

"I know," said Heidi as she dropped the bracelet into her pocket. "All I need is a little magic."

Chapter 7

A BAD MIX

Heidi sat on her bed and opened her *Book of Spells*. She ran her finger down the page and found a section called Jewelry Repair. *Perfect,* she thought as she flipped to the page.

She read over the spell:

77

Jewelry Repair

Has your favorite piece of jewelry been broken? Have you busted a clasp? Lost a gemstone? Perhaps you've damaged a charm or locket? Then this is the spell for you!

Ingredients:
1 cup of apple juice
1 teaspoon of sugar
2 grape seeds

Collect the ingredients and mix them together in a glass. Add the broken jewelry. Hold your Witches of Westwick medallion in one hand and place your other hand over the mix. Chant the following words:

JINGLE, JAGGLE, JIGGLE!
WATCH THIS [PIECE OF JEWELRY] WIGGLE!
MAKE IT LOOK AS GOOD AS NEW
WITHOUT STAPLES, STRING, OR GLUE!

I can make Mom's bracelet as good as new, Heidi said to herself. She hopped off her bed and ran to the kitchen. Then she helped herself to a cup of apple juice, a mixing spoon, and two grapes. *Now all I need is some sugar.*

Mom had left a bowl of red sugar on the counter. She had been making Christmas cookies. Heidi sprinkled a teaspoon of red sugar into the glass with the apple juice. Then she snuck everything to her room.

Heidi shut her bedroom door and sat at her desk. First she nibbled half a grape. Then she picked out the seeds with her finger-nail and dropped two into the glass. Heidi stirred the ingredients with the spoon.

Next she added the smooshed bracelet. She held the medallion in her right hand and put her left hand over the mix.

Heidi chanted the spell.
The mix bubbled, and
the bracelet wiggled
and jiggled. Heidi waited
for the liquid to settle. Then she
fished out the bracelet.

The charms had been perfectly
repaired, but there was just one small
problem: The bracelet was covered in
rust.

SOMETHiNG FiSHY

Uh-oh, thought Heidi. *I totally messed up.* She shoved the bracelet into her jeans pocket and ran into the kitchen. *There's only one person who can help me now.*

"Mom, can I go to Aunt Trudy's?" Heidi asked.

Mom gave her a *what are you up to now?* look.

"I need to talk to her about a Christmas surprise," explained Heidi.

"Well, okay," Mom said. "Be back before dinner."

Heidi pulled on her boots and coat and raced to her aunt's house. Aunt

Trudy answered the door and smiled. Her cats, Agnes and Hilda, swirled beneath her flowing purple skirt.

"What a lovely surprise!" said Aunt Trudy. "Is something the matter?"

"How did you know?" asked Heidi.

"Just a hunch," said Aunt Trudy. "Come on in."

Heidi followed her aunt to the kitchen and sat at the table. The house smelled like ginger.

"Would you like a slice of ginger-bread?" asked Aunt Trudy.

"I'd love one," said Heidi.

Aunt Trudy set the gingerbread and a glass of milk in front of Heidi. Then she sat down across from her. After taking a bite of gingerbread, Heidi reached into her pocket and pulled out the rusty charm bracelet.

"Oh my," said Aunt Trudy. "Is that your mother's charm bracelet?"

Heidi nodded.

She told her aunt about how she had taken the bracelet without asking and about how it had gotten run over by the snowplow.

"I used a jewelry repair spell," said Heidi. "But something went wrong."

"I see," said Aunt Trudy. "What kind of sugar did you use?"

"Red Christmas sugar," said Heidi.

"Well, that explains the rust," said Aunt Trudy.

"Can we fix it?" asked Heidi.

"We can," said Aunt Trudy. "But we'll need silver

fish scales, and they have to be special ordered. They'd take about six weeks to get here."

"Six weeks!" said Heidi. "What if Mom finds out about the bracelet before then?"

"Well, maybe you should tell her what happened," Aunt Trudy suggested.

"Are you kidding?" said Heidi. "She'll be so mad at me. I took it without asking."

"We all make mistakes, honey," said Aunt Trudy. "Your mom may get cross, but she'll understand."

Heidi stared at the rusty bracelet.
Her stomach felt queasy. The gingerbread gurgled in her tummy.

"Think about it," said Aunt Trudy
with a wink.

Heidi gave her aunt a big hug and then plodded through the snow toward home. She looked at the bright Christmas lights on the trees and houses. She passed by a brightly lit Santa holding an armful of presents. Heidi sighed. *Santa will be so disappointed in me.* Then Heidi stopped in her tracks. *On second thought, maybe Santa can help me.*

Chapter 9

A HOLLY JOLLY FAVOR

Heidi sat on her bed and began to write another letter.

Hi, Santa,

It's me again. Christmas is two days away, and guess

97

what? I was BAD! I borrowed my mom's charm bracelet to play dress-up without asking for her permission.

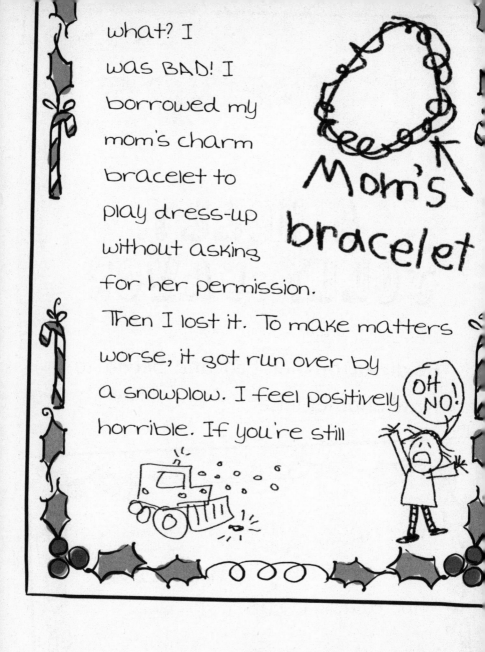

Then I lost it. To make matters worse, it got run over by a snowplow. I feel positively horrible. If you're still

OH NO!

reading this, I want to ask you a favor. Will you please bring me a new charm bracelet instead of the book I asked for? I want to give the bracelet to my mom. Since I was bad, you don't have to bring me PRINCESS CHARMING. Thanks.

Your friend,

Heidi

PS This won't happen again. I promise.

MY MOM

Heidi put the letter in the mailbox and sighed. *Santa probably won't get my letter in time, but what else can I do?* she thought. She kicked a chunk of snow on the way up the front walk. *Wait! Maybe there IS something else I can*

do. I can make Mom a special bracelet for Christmas in case Santa doesn't send the charm bracelet in time.

Heidi hurried inside and pulled out her bead kit. She strung rainbow crystals and a few of her fanciest stones on a piece of memory wire. Dad helped with the clasp. Heidi laid

the finished bracelet on her bed. *This is the prettiest bracelet I've ever made,* she thought. She wrapped it in red tissue paper and stuck a small white bow on top. Then she hurried downstairs and tucked it under the tree.

Chapter 10

CHRiSTMAS MAGiC

"Hooray! It's Christmas!" shouted Henry. "Time to get up!"

Henry pounced on Heidi. Then he woke up Mom and Dad.

"Let's open presents!" he said.

"You may open your stocking stuffers," said Mom. "We'll open tree presents when Aunt Trudy gets here."

Heidi and Henry unhooked their stockings from the mantel. Then they sat down and took turns calling out their presents—a family tradition.

"I got Hot Wheels!" shouted Henry.

"I got some fake tattoos!" cried Heidi.

They unwrapped jacks, scented erasers and pencils, sports cards, snow globes, Silly Putty, fuzzy toe socks, and chocolate Santas.

Aunt Trudy joined them for coffee cake, scrambled eggs, and bacon. Then they opened the presents from under the tree. Everyone took turns. Heidi paid close attention to what Mom opened.

Soon there were just a few presents left. Mom still hadn't opened the bracelet Heidi made, and

that was the only present she had left
to open. Heidi only had one present
to go too, and it was her turn to open.
I really hope this is the charm bracelet,
she thought.

It was a present from Santa! Heidi tore off the paper and found *Princess Charming*, the book she had wanted earlier. *Drat,* she thought. *Santa didn't get my letter in time.* Now she would have to tell her mom what had happened.

She waited until it was Mom's turn again. Mom unwrapped the hand-made bracelet. Then Dad fastened it on Mom's wrist.

"I love it," Mom said.

Mom kissed Heidi on the cheek.

"There's a little story that goes with it," said Heidi.

Heidi took a deep breath and told her mother about the charm bracelet. She told her how she had lost it, how she tried to fix it, and how she had written to Santa in hopes of getting a new one.

"I'm so sorry," Heidi said.

Mom gave Heidi a big squeeze.

"Well, I'm sorry too," she said. "But I like the bracelet you made for me even better. It's a Heidi original."

"Then you're not mad?" asked Heidi.

"No, I'm not mad," said Mom. "I've

been saving the bracelet for you. Losing it taught you a lesson about taking something without asking."

"No kidding," said Heidi.

Then Henry pulled something from one of the tree's branches.

"Hey, look what I found!" he said.

Everyone looked at what Henry had in his hand.

"What . . . ?" asked Dad.

"Is that . . . ?" started Mom.

"Your charm bracelet!" exclaimed Heidi. She grabbed the bracelet from Henry. "The rust is all gone!"

Mom looked at Aunt Trudy. "Did you have something to do with this?" she asked suspiciously.

"I wish I had," said Aunt Trudy. "But it wasn't me."

"Then how did the bracelet wind up on our tree?" asked Dad.

Heidi's eyes lit up. "It must've been Santa!" she exclaimed.

"Well, duh," said Henry. "Who else could it have been?"

Then everyone became very quiet.

"Wow," said Heidi. "This must be Christmas magic."

And they all knew that something very special had taken place.

Ho, ho, ho!

119

Check out the next book starring

HEiDi
HECKELBECK

Boing! Boing! Boing!

No one could sit still in Mrs. Welli's classroom. Everyone wanted to hold Maggie. Maggie was a fluffy white bunny with bright blue eyes. She belonged to Principal Pennypacker, but sometimes he let Maggie go on classroom visits.

This week Mrs. Welli's class had

An excerpt from *Heidi Heckelbeck and the Tie-Dyed Bunny*

Maggie. Mrs. Welli let her students take turns holding the bunny. When it was Heidi's turn, she cuddled Maggie in her arms. The other kids gathered around.

"Her fur feels like velvet," said Heidi.

Lucy Lancaster stroked Maggie's fur. "She's the softest little fluff ball in the whole world," she said.

Mrs. Welli clapped her hands.

"Everyone, take your seats," she said. "It's time to put Maggie back in her cage. The bunny needs a rest."

Heidi slowly walked to the cage and

let Maggie hop in. Then she sat down with the rest of the class.

"I have very exciting news, boys and girls," Mrs. Welli said. "Principal Pennypacker is going to pick one lucky boy or girl to take Maggie home for Easter weekend."

Everyone gasped and squealed.

"At the end of the day," Mrs. Welli continued, "the principal will draw a name from our class hat."

Everyone began to chatter about who would get the bunny. Heidi had always dreamed of having her very own pet. *Oh, I hope I'll get the bunny.*

An excerpt from *Heidi Heckelbeck and the Tie-Dyed Bunny*